CHAI & CANVAS

RAGI UNNIKRISHNAN

Made with ♥ on the Notion Press Platform
www.notionpress.com

Contents

To my father, whose boundless creativity and love for storytelling inspired me to pick up the pen. Every word I write is infused with your creativity.

And to my daughter,

For her unwavering love and support. Your belief in me gives me strength, and your light brightens every corner of my life.

This anthology is for you both — my greatest inspirations.

With all my love,
Ragi

PAINTING A PROMISE

Dear Readers,

Welcome to Painting a Promise, a story about love, grief, and the transformational power of art. The story is set against the vibrant and soulful backdrop of Thrissur.

As you start your journey with Dev and Gowri, you'll find layers within their narrative—a tribute to those we have lost, a celebration of the connections we discover, and a reminder that new beginnings often rise from the ashes of sorrow. Pay attention to the walls, the rain, and the eyes of a painted woman, for they hold the keys to understanding the deeper story within.

This tale tells us about rediscovery and healing through love. It's also about finding beauty in the present moment.

Thanks for taking this path with them and letting the colors speak to you. I hope their story lingers long after you've read the book.

1

The Forgotten Pathway

At the center of Kerala's warm embrace is Thrissur, where temples tell stories that go beyond time and space. Once again, the city is bustling under the warm glow of Pooram's light. A place where art and faith come together, Thrissivaperur, aka Thrissur. Dev was standing in the heart of Thrissur, a town he knew all too well. Drums played, events with lots of color, and busy streets full of people. But for him, it seemed far away, like a dream that was ending. Now, his mind was empty, but it used to be full of artistic thoughts. That man used to paint lots of wonderful art forms, but now there's nothing. He got lost in the town and didn't know where to go. It seemed like the world was moving without him. It had been two years since he lost Nandini. She was his first love, she was his friend, and she was his inspiration. Dev had trouble getting back to life or his art after she died. His heart felt empty without her there, and nothing seemed to fill it.

It was getting dark outside, and it looked like it was going to rain. Dev was walking through the old streets of Thrissur. The normal chaos and noise of Pooram were a long way away. Cities seemed to be waiting for something as they became quieter. He walked down a tiny, forgotten path. Moss grew on both sides of the walls, and the gates were so rusted that they barely hung on their hinges. It looked like time had forgotten about this spot. It seemed like the world had stopped here because everything was still. He then saw it. Behind vines and other plants is a wall. He first thought it was just an old wall, but as he got closer, he saw that it was actually a painting that was only partly painted. Something about it caught his eye, even though the colors were faded from age.

The painting was of a woman, though she was only partially painted. She wasn't a real woman, but a figure of his dreams, a mix of love and longing that spoke to his heart. Her eyes, though incomplete, held something deep—sadness, hope, or perhaps both. Her eyes had a quiet focus that made him think she knew more than she let on, but she was still lost in the unfinished lines of the painting. Dev just stood there and gazed at the picture. He thought it was talking to him and was part of his own story. With all the memories in his heart, there was also a spark of something new, a motivation he hadn't felt in years.

Dev gently touched the wall; the paint was rough. He felt the painting was waiting for long to get finished. At that very moment, Dev felt something change inside him. He thought, "Maybe this is where I start over." He was here because of the lost path, and he knew what he needed to do now. To honor the past and maybe find something new, he would paint again. This time, it wasn't just to fill the void. Dev took a step back because the moment felt heavy. With each brushstroke, he filled in the blank areas where the woman's figure had previously been indistinct and unclear. He put everything he had into the painting; every color and shape showed how he felt. It was no longer just sadness that was showing in the woman's eyes; they were now clear. He didn't just make the painting; it revealed his own soul, caught in the rhythm of the paint. With the last touch, the woman on the wall seemed to breathe, and Dev's image of her unfinished story came to life.

2

A Whisper of Connection

Gowri didn't have any specific plans when she got to Thrissur; she just wanted to see all of Kerala's hidden gems. She really enjoyed the idea of finding beauty in the most remote spots that no one else seemed to notice. She had been to many towns and many cities, but something about Thrissur felt different. It wasn't the grand temples or the festivals, though they were mesmerizing; it was the old streets, the forgotten paths, the stories that lingered in the shadows. She walked around the quieter roads near Thekkinkadu Maidhanam on her second day. A few blocks away were the busy streets, but everything felt calm here.

The walls were old, with shades that were fading like memories. The air smelled like wet earth after it had rained. She found something she didn't expect in one of these hidden passageways. At first, she thought it was just an old forgotten wall covered in grass. She then saw it: the picture. Newly painted colors told a tale from behind the bushes. A painting of a woman, soft yet haunting, stared back at her. Her eyes were full of longing as if she had a story to tell, a story that no one had ever heard. Gowri couldn't look away. There was something about her, something familiar yet strange. She moved closer, and her fingers touched the wall's wet surface. The woman in the picture came to life for a moment, as if she was ready for Gowri to understand her story. Gowri had a strong feeling of connection to the woman in the painting, but she couldn't explain why. The picture seemed to communicate to her in a manner she couldn't quite understand but could feel. When she bent down to look more closely, she saw a line written at the bottom of the picture.

The words were in Malayalam and were simple and haunting:

"Orikkalum kandumuttanidayillatha ente pranayathinu."

(For the love I may never meet).

The words hit her hard; she remained gazing at the painting for a long time. She didn't know why, but she felt like she had to know more about this painting, about the person who painted it. The painting was hiding a story, a quiet ache, and she felt an urge to find out what it was. Then Gowri decided to find the artist. After seeing the painting and reading the lines, she felt an unsettling sensation in her chest. She walked away from the painting with a new sense of purpose. She was determined to find out more about the artist who had put so much of himself into this wall on a neglected pathway.

3

Tracing the Colours

Gowri's search began to wind its way through the town of Thrissur, and the days went by quickly. She went to well-known art galleries and stopped to look at the work of local artists, but the paintings she saw had a raw feeling and were better than anything she saw there. It had a mysterious feel to it like there was a quiet magic that couldn't be explained.

She spoke with people in the area about the artwork she discovered. A lot of people had seen and heard about it, but few knew who created it. Many were unaware of the artist's story. Some people said he lived alone and was well-known for his artwork. Some people said he had stopped painting completely after losing a loved one. It was not clear what had happened, but everyone agreed that he was no longer seen in public. Things got even more interesting for Gowri. She spent her days sitting in neighborhood coffee shops, speaking with people who might know something about the mysterious artist.

She learned that his name was Dev. Some said his house was near the Vadakkumnathan Temple, a place where he had lived alone for as long as anyone could remember. One evening, she sat across from an older guy who sold tea. When she asked about Dev, he looked at her with serious thought. He said, "Ah, Dev," slowly, and his wrinkled face softened as he reflected on him. "No one else could paint like him." His art had a lot of life in it. In every stroke, you could see his heart. Then... something took place. He stopped. Now he's just a shadow of himself, cutting himself off from everyone else.

Gowri felt sad when he spoke those words. She knew what it was like to lose someone and how it could quieten your soul and take away your colors. She didn't understand why this man, this artist, had pulled away so much. What did he lose? And was that same loss that the painting she found was based on? Instead of just being interested, her search for him turned into a way to figure out what the colors on the wall meant and what feelings they had soaked into them. Gowri knew she had to talk to him and find him. That's when she chose to try something new. She chose to go to places where artists might meet instead of asking around town again. She visited local tea shops, quiet stores, or secret gardens with walls covered in sketches and unfinished projects. She needed to know more about Dev and the guy he used to be. After a lot of searching, she found a small area of Thrissur hidden between some busy streets and a temple. The room was quiet and smelled like old books and plants. There, she found a small art shop. When she said Dev's name, the man behind the counter, who was also an artist, smiled. "I used to see him here, lost in thought and drawing in the corner. That was a long time ago, though. I haven't seen him in a long time. Some say he still lives in the house he used to live in near the temple, but no one is sure. He stays by himself."

Gowri knew she was only one step away from finding him. It was clear to her. She was drawn to him by the connection she felt with the painting. As she walked through the streets of Thrissur that evening, the sounds of the city faded into the background. The rhythm of her footsteps matched the steady beat of her heart. The artwork had become a part of her, and she was desperate to locate the artist who created it. She intended to look for his residence near Vadakkumnathan Temple the following day. That was the only place she could think to look for the person who had painted the woman on the wall. She had no idea that the woman's narrative had only begun to resemble her own.

4

A Twist of Fate

The sky was dark with clouds as Gowri walked toward Vadakkumnathan Temple the next day. She heard from some locals about Dev's house being nearby, but no one could tell her exactly where to find it. So she walked along the narrow lanes, her footsteps echoing in the silence. The temple, with its serene environment and majestic arches, reflected positive hopes. Optimism was floating in the air. Gowri walked past the temple gates, looking for clues to the artist's location. As she was about to walk into another narrow road, a torrential rainfall began and quickly engulfed everything. She rushed to the nearest shelter, a little chai store at the alley's corner. The sign over the door read Chai & Canvas, which is recognized for its friendly atmosphere among local artists. The pleasant aroma of spices and tea filled the air. The shop had a uniqueness to it and was welcoming. The walls of the shop were covered in paintings, drawings, and pictures, some of which were unfinished as if the artists had left a piece of themselves in the room. Gowri took a seat beside the window, hoping the rain would stop soon. While looking around the room, she noticed a few people, but one guy caught her attention. He was seated in the corner, a notebook open in front of him, and his pencil was moving quickly over the page. Gowri's eyes remained fixed. There was something familiar about him, but she couldn't identify it. Perhaps it was the way he held himself or the intensity in his look that reminded her of the guy who could have created the painting. She was about to look away when their eyes met. The sound of the rain appeared to fade into the distance as time seemed to stretch for a while. Neither of them spoke a word, yet there seemed to be an unspoken connection, an instant understanding. The spell was broken, and he returned his focus to his sketchbook, unconscious of the pull he had just generated.

Gowri hesitated for a moment, then stood up, her heart racing. She walked over to the counter and ordered a cup of chai, stealing another glance at the man in the corner. He looked so immersed in his art, so distant from the world around him, but there was something about him that felt so real. She couldn't ignore the feeling that she had seen him before.

When her chai arrived, she found a seat near the back, watching the rain tap against the window. The storm outside raged on, but inside, the tea shop was warm and quiet. As she sipped her tea, she noticed that the man in the corner had finally set down his pencil. He stretched, glancing around the room as if looking for something. His eyes met hers again.

This time he smiled. He was hesitant to smile as if he had forgotten to smile. "Seems like the rain isn't stopping," he said, his voice low but steady. Gowri smiled back,

"It doesn't look like it. It's funny how rain can make the world seem so still." He nodded, his eyes remaining focused. "I get what you mean. Sometimes the world outside slips away, leaving you with only your thoughts."

"Or your artwork." Gowri felt a sense of recognition. She had come here looking for an artist. She had come to find the man who painted the artwork, the one whose heartache and longing had drawn her in. Could this be him? She leaned forward slightly, her curiosity bubbling up. "I've been wondering... do you know the mural near Thekkinkadu Maidhanam? The one featuring a painting of a woman. The woman in the picture has magical eyes that are full of feelings." The man's face changed as she mentioned the artwork. An expression of surprise flashed through his face, followed by a shadow of something else, unreadable. "Are you talking about the one on the old wall?" he asked, his voice quieter now. Gowri nodded, watching his reaction closely. "Yes, that's the one. I've been looking for the artist. Do you know who painted it?" The man paused, his hand resting on his cup of chai as if weighing his words. He looked around the shop, concentrating on the door to make sure no one was listening. "Actually... I do," he said gently, returning his focus to her. "I'm the one who painted it."

Gowri felt her heart skip a beat. She had found him. The artist—the man whose grief and passion echoed in the painting. He was sitting in front of her. She hadn't expected it to happen this way, not in the middle of a downpour, not in a quiet teashop with the world outside buried by a curtain of rain. For a minute, neither of them spoke. The rain outside appeared to rage louder, but inside, everything was still, as if the two of them were the only ones in the world. Then, as if a new chapter had begun, Gowri broke the silence. “I’ve been waiting to understand it,” she murmured softly. “There’s something about the painting that drew me in. And I believe it has reached out to you as well.” Dev stared at her, his eyes softening with what may have been a relief. “Maybe,” she replied softly.

5

Unveiling the Story

The rain had finally subsided to a light drizzle by the time Gowri and Dev left the tea shop. The air was dense with the earthy aroma of moist earth, and the streets of Thrissur were illuminated by the mellow glow of streetlamps. Neither of them talked as they walked side by side, their shoes echoing across the calm streets. Dev led the way without speaking, his pace sluggish but consistent. Gowri followed. She had finally identified the artist, the man responsible for the artwork. The person who put all of his heart into that wall and made something so beautiful and full of desire. It hit her hard, as she walked behind him, what was going on. She wasn't just meeting the artist; she was meeting the man whose feelings and pain led him to paint. They got to a small road close to the temple. The houses there were old and the walls were worn down. They appeared to lean toward one another as if they were exchanging secrets that only the walls could hear. At the end of the street, hidden behind a giant banyan tree, was a small home. It wasn't fancy, but something was reassuring about it.

Dev stopped in front of the gate and looked at Gowri. "This is where I live," he said in a low voice that was hard to hear. There were echoes of the past in the air, and history could be seen in the walls. "Want to come inside?" asked Dev. "I really need to tell you a story." Gowri was excited. This was the moment she had been waiting for—the moment Dev would finally speak of the story behind the painting and the emotions that inspired him to paint something so longing and raw. The house was calm inside, with the kind of serenity that can only come from solitude. The walls were covered with ancient paintings, incomplete sketches, and strewn canvases.

The *netipattam* seemed unusual, with peacock feathers attached to its ends. It was evident that this location had once been vibrant with innovation but seemed trapped in time. Dev took her to a small room at the back of the home, where a wooden easel lay in the corner, surrounded by old paintbrushes and blank canvases. The room smelled of paint and years of incomplete work. Dev walked to a little table in the corner and took out a battered sketchbook.

"Nandini," he said with an ache in his voice, opening the book to a page filled with sketches of a woman—her face, her hair, her eyes. Gowri recognized the features immediately. It resembled the woman from the mural, the one who had called to her. But these drawings were different. They had a softness and depth that the painting didn't have.

His voice was barely above a whisper as he said, "Her name was Nandini. I liked her a lot. My inspiration, my everything. She's gone now," he paused, "She died." He took a moment to think about what he was going to say because the thought of her name made the past heavy.

It made Gowri's heart race. She wasn't ready for this. She thought Nandini was just a memory, a love he had lost. It was clear that the loss was still fresh when she heard the pain and sadness in Dev's voice. Nandini wasn't just a memory from the past; she was a part of him, lodged deep in his being.

"She was my closest friend," Dev continued, his eyes distant as he looked at the sketches. "We grew up together. We shared everything, our dreams, our fears. I loved her, Gowri. More than anything." His voice cracked slightly, and Gowri could see the pain in his eyes. She reached out, placing a gentle hand on his arm, offering him the comfort of her presence.

"I thought I could move on," Dev murmured. He turned away from the drawings and out the window, it was raining again. "I couldn't, though. It seemed like the world lost its color when she died. That painting was something I did to remember her and hold on to what was lost. The woman in the painting isn't Nandini exactly, but she represents everything I wish I could've had, everything that was taken away."

Gowri's heart ached for him. The weight of his loss and the depth of his sadness were clear to her. It looked like Dev had put all of his unspoken love and sadness into that painting, making something beautiful but also very deep.

Gowri asked, "And the words at the bottom that read 'For the love I may never meet'—that's for her, right?"

It was an overwhelming memory for Dev, and it made his eyes dark. "Yes. It is for Nandini. Because I never got to claim her love. For the love that was taken away too soon."

It was very quiet in the room for a long time while it rained outside. Gowri could feel sadness in the air, and she knew it would never go away from him. Nandini had been a part of his life, and now, she was a part of his grief. But something about Dev's pain seemed to be shifting, as though, in the telling of this story, a part of him was letting go.

"There's something else," he whispered. "I held onto something that was leaving me while I was painting. Now I know it's time to let go. It was time to leave the past behind."

Gowri was stunned by the weight of his words as she looked at him. She knew what it was like to be hurt and lose someone close to you. Now she understood that Dev's journey wasn't just about remembering Nandini but also about getting better and moving on.

Dev said, "I don't know how," and his voice shook a little. "But I need to get back to life. To paint once more."

Gowri could feel the warmth rising in her chest. In her heart, she knew that this was the time when Dev would finally start to get better. She wasn't sure what the future held, but she was sure that they had both found something in this quiet room full of memories.

She said, “Maybe we can paint something together. Something that helps you move on. Finding hope after the worst losses.”

Dev was looking at her, trying to read her mind. He smiled after a long time. There was a hint of something new in his guarded smile.

“Maybe,” Dev said.

Exactly at that moment, Gowri knew things would be different for them in the future. Through the art of loss and remembering, they found each other. Now, maybe they could make something new that would bring color back to their lives.

6

The Muse Found

The days that followed were more tranquil than usual, but there was a subtle change in the atmosphere, akin to the first breath of morning after a long night. As Gowri and Dev spent more time together, their conversations got deeper and more in-depth, going beyond art and loss. But in the times they were silent together, there was a link that had been developing gradually between them since the first time they met.

Dev started to sketch again, his hands trembling at first, as if they were remembering the motion of creation. The first few lines were uncertain and wary, but as the days progressed, the strokes became more confident and proficient. Gowri observed him closely. She was always there in a composed manner that appeared to provide him exactly the right balance of space and encouragement.

One evening, Dev invited Gowri back along the forgotten path. The temple bells rang with a soft, steady chime. The sky had a hue of orange. They walked side by side. There was a new liveliness between them, an invisible thread bringing them closer than before.

When they arrived at the wall, Dev stood for a moment, silently looking at the mural. Gowri could sense ideas whirling in his mind. The painting always portrayed loss, a tribute to Nandini that left no place for anything else. But there was something odd about the air as they stood before it now. The painting seemed like it had been waiting for this time as well, to change and evolve.

“This is where it all started,” Dev said, his voice almost a whisper.

Gowri nodded, her gaze falling on the familiar figure of the woman in the mural, her face half hidden in shadow, a reflection of a love that had never been. But now the artwork no longer caused the same grief it once did. Rather, it seemed to be a promise.

“I think it’s time,” Dev said, looking at Gowri. “I have decided to paint, not only for me but also for us. For what’s to come.”

Gowri felt a comforting warmth in his words. She could feel the weight of his words, and she realized what they meant. This wasn’t just about a painting; it was about reclaiming life and finding beauty in a world that once seemed ruined.

“I’m ready if you are,” she said, her voice steady, her heart full of excitement.

Together, they stood there, surrounded by the stillness of the evening, and the quiet hum of the town in the distance. Dev picked up a paintbrush, the familiar weight of it feeling right in his hand, and began to work. Gowri watched him; something unspoken in her heart started to expand. She felt his misery, but she also could see hope rising to shape his strokes.

Dev painted for hours. He painted layer after layer of the painting, mixing colors that appeared to pulse with new life. Gowri stood by, occasionally suggesting something and other times just enjoying the beauty right in front of her. And as the night became darker, something amazing started to show itself—a figure very unlike the woman in the previous painting, but now her face was brighter, more vivid, as though she had come alive on the canvas. Once covered with sadness, her eyes now radiated a gentle energy. Her facial lines were softer and broader as if she were no longer a dream or recollection but something real.

When the final stroke was placed, both of them stepped back to evaluate the work. The painting had evolved into something very distinct. Once expressing Dev's loss, the lady now stood as a symbol of hope, of rebirth, of the calm strength that had grown from the darkest distress.

Looking at the painting, Dev exclaimed, "This is it," his voice full of joy. There was a lightness in his voice, a release that had been absent before. "This is what I was meant to paint."

Gowri looked at the mural, her heart swelling with pride for the man beside her. She had never expected that an encounter with a painting would lead her here—to this moment, to this journey. As she stood in front of the wall, cool air on her skin, she felt a deep feeling of calm. They had both discovered something new. Something that was theirs to share.

Dev looked at her, his eyes full of gratitude. "Thank you," he said softly, his voice full of emotion. "Thank you for being here. For being a part of it."

Gowri smiled. "You don't need to thank me. We are in this together."

The painting was no longer a tribute to his past. It was a mirror of his current state of mind, his road toward healing. It was proof that, even after loss, healing is possible and life can be beautiful.

As they stood side by side, the painting behind them gleaming in the gentle moonlight, they realized their story had just begun. What had previously been a forgotten path, hidden away from the world, is now a beacon of light, hope, and love.

A new chapter had begun, not just for Dev and Gowri, but for the painting, too. It will continue to tell its story, not just of longing, but of the quiet power of moving forward, of healing, and of the unexpected ways in which love could bloom again.

7

A New Beginning

The world around them changed. The forgotten path, once buried in shadows and silence, had become a vibrant place. The painting, with its bright hues and new details, had become a symbol of something intense—a reflection of Dev and Gowri's journey together. It was no longer just a work of art; it was a tale of love, healing, and two hearts meeting in the most unforeseen circumstances. Every time they stopped to see the picture, it seemed like they were experiencing a dream. The way their eyes met showed that they understood each other without having to say a word.

Gowri had become his anchor. In her company, the world appeared brighter, and the weight of the past no longer lingered on him. Every look she gave him, her soft smile, made him feel as if he could finally see the world in color again. She was more than just the muse who reignited his love of painting; she had become the muse of his heart.

One evening, Dev and Gowri stood in front of the painting. The cool evening breeze blew around them, lifting her hair, and everything else faded. It was just the two of them, standing together in the soft glow of the sunset.

Dev turned to Gowri, "I never thought I'd feel this way again." His words carried the weight of all he had gone through and rediscovered in her. "You've made everything seem... possible." Gowri looked up at him, her heart racing. He spoke with such tenderness that it felt as if he were confessing not just his feelings, but his entire soul. She reached out and softly touched his cheek as if to ground herself in the reality of the situation.

Gowri's voice was filled with passion; she said, "You have always had the power within you. I just helped you see it."

He smiled, but his eyes were deeper now. "No, Gowri. You have shown me what it means to live and love again." His hand moved to cup her face gently. "I didn't know I needed you. But now, I can't imagine life without you."

The world seemed to hold its breath as they stood there, inches apart, hearts racing, waiting. Gowri felt the warmth of his touch, filling the space between them with an irresistible draw, an energy she could no longer ignore. She took a step forward, the distance between them narrowing until there were only the two of them and the possibility of something more.

"I feel the same way," she murmured, her voice barely a whisper. "I've never met anyone who could make me feel so... alive, so complete." Her hand moved to his chest, resting there. "You've shown me that love isn't just a dream—it's real; it's right here, with you." And then, as if the universe itself had conspired to bring them together, Dev leaned in, his lips brushing against hers with a tenderness that took her breath away. It was a kiss that spoke of longing, of loss, and of the healing power of love. It was soft at first as if testing the waters, but as the seconds stretched into eternity, it deepened, filled with a passion that had been waiting to be set free.

When they pulled away, breathless and trembling, the world around them seemed to glow brighter. The painting behind them bathed in the fading light of the sunset, had transformed from a symbol of longing to a symbol of love—a love that had bloomed against all odds, a love that had found its way through the cracks of time and pain.

Dev looked at her, his eyes filled with a warmth she had never seen before. "You're everything I never realized I needed." Tears welled up in her eyes, but they were tears of joy, of something so pure and real that it felt like a dream. She kissed him again, this time with all the love and gratitude in her heart. She didn't need to say the words; everything they needed to communicate was in that kiss, in the way their hearts beat in time with each other. And when the sun eventually dropped below the horizon, leaving the world bathed in the warm glow of sunset, they stood there, hand in hand, their future unfolding before them.

The painting, now a tribute to their journey, would always remind them of how far they had come—how love had healed them both, how it had brought them from the darkness into the light. At that moment, they understood that their tale was far from done. It had just begun. And whatever challenges the world would throw their way, they would face them together—side by side, heart to heart. The forgotten pathway, once a place of solitude, had become their sanctuary, their home. And there, among the colors and memories they had painted together, love had found its place. It would be remembered forever.

AROMA OF TRUTH

At its core, the story is beyond betrayal or loss; it's about finding yourself, endurance, and one's own strength. Meera's story reflects so many unseen stories—of women who find courage amid hardship and reframe their own narratives when life throws them a curveball.

As you immerse yourself in Meera's world, keep an eye out for the little details: the aroma of her cooking, the quiet strength in her silences, and the evolving colors of her world. These are more than just elements of the story—they hint at her transformation. Her journey reminds us what life may throw at us and it is in rebuilding that we truly discover ourselves.

Hope it resonates with you, inspires you, and reminds you of the immense strength we all possess.

With love and gratitude,
Ragi

8

Meera's Musings

My name is Meera, and if you were to ask anyone in this small town of ours, they'd probably tell you that I'm the typical housewife. Not that I mind. After all, it's a title that comes with a lot of perks, like endless compliments about my cooking and the kind of unsolicited advice from aunties who, despite decades of experience in matrimony and child-rearing, still manage to act as though I'm just one tempering of mustard seeds away from ruining my family.

Take Raghavan, my husband. Oh, I've spent years perfecting the art of domesticity, and he never fails to remind me of how lucky he is. "Meera, you're the backbone of our family," he'll say, taking a slow sip of his tea. The one thing, according to him, no one else can prepare just the way he likes. It's almost as if he believes that domestic bliss is something that simply happens without any effort. No, not a single thought to the fact that I am, in fact, a wizard in the kitchen, a food magician who conjures perfectly crispy dosas from the same batter that could be used to glue a small building together. But that's fine. I do not mind. After all, a woman who can make a meal appear out of thin air is not just an illusionist, she is, in the eyes of society, an ideal.

Each day begins with the thought of my husband and kids leaving at just the right time. Because, honestly, nothing screams 'I've got my life together' more than waking up long before it makes any sense. The kids, Lakshmi and Arun, bless their hearts, are still asleep, wrapped up in their world of schoolbooks and video games, unaware of the gourmet masterpieces I am crafting just for them. I take a few moments to revel in my own competence as I grind fresh coconut, expertly chop vegetables, and prepare sambar with the kind of focus that would make a surgeon jealous. "No one is as good as you when it comes to cooking," Raghavan always says. And I, like any housewife, pretend to be humble, but inside, I'm elated with joy as if I'm awarded the MasterChef Trophy.

So, I'm sitting there, folding the freshly pressed shirts (I don't know why we have so many shirts, he only wears three of them, but we have fourteen), when I start to realize something odd. Raghavan is spending a little more time "at work" lately, and when he does come home, he's always "so tired", as if the office has suddenly decided that it's a high-stakes war zone. For a moment, I feel a flicker of doubt. But then I remember, he is my husband. He wouldn't. He's not that kind of man. He's the kind of man who eats my sambar with a smile, who calls me "the best cook in the world." Surely, I have nothing to worry about.

And yet, there I was wondering if the scent of perfume clinging to his collar was just a result of one too many mornings in the office air conditioning. Maybe it was a new cologne, or my perfect life was about to be flipped upside down in a way that no perfectly spiced curry could ever fix.

9

A Whiff of Doubt

Let me tell you something about men. They don't change. Raghavan, for instance, has been Raghavan since the day we met. He likes his tea just perfect. He reads the newspaper from front to back, completely ignoring the sections that matter. And, of course, he likes his meals just so, not too much spice, not too little.

But let's be honest, he's predictable. He's always home by 7:30 PM, never later. Always on time. And if he's not, I don't need to worry. I've got everything under control. My dinner is ready, the kids are bathed, and the house smells like the perfect blend of coconut and curry leaves. Meera the Magnificent, who else would manage it all with such grace?

Except, of course, for that one evening.

It was a Tuesday, because, of course, it had to be a Tuesday. I'd already set the table for the three of us, since Arun was off at a friend's place and Lakshmi was deep in her study hole, preparing for yet another exam that was clearly going to determine her entire future.

Raghavan wasn't home yet, but I wasn't worried. He was probably just finishing up a late meeting. My husband, the workaholic, what else could it be?

But then, 7:45 PM came. And then 8:00 PM. I could hear my favorite Sundari Kannal song from the living room, but my mind was fixated on the ticking clock. You see, I'm a woman of routine. And when that routine is disrupted, something deep inside me starts to twitch.

By 8:30 PM, I was getting worried. But not too worried. After all, I am Meera, a woman who can whip up a three-course meal with one hand while juggling the world with the other. A little lateness wasn't going to throw me off. My hands were restless, and I felt a strange pressure building in my chest.

Then, just as I was about to dial his number, the doorbell rang. Ah, I thought. "Here he is. Raghavan is finally home."

But no, it wasn't Raghavan. It was our neighbor, Aunty BBC of the society, Anasuya, with a sheepish grin plastered on her face.

"Is Raghavan at home?" she asked, her voice laced with sweet venom, her sharp eyes darting around as if she were searching for proof of some hidden scandal.

"No," I said, forcing a smile that felt as brittle as the biscuit in her hand, "but he'll be home soon."

"Oh, is that so?" she said, tilting her head dramatically, the faintest smirk tugging at her lips. "Well, you might want to let him know that Priya was looking for him."

"Priya? Who?"

Not missing a beat, she leaned in slightly, lowering her voice to a stage whisper that could still be heard by half the building. "She's new to the building, isn't she? Works with him, I believe. I've seen him leaving her flat quite a few times, mind you. Oh, I thought you'd know, being family friends and all."

Her smile grew wider as she stepped back, concealing the joy within her as the weight of her words lingered in the air.

Priya. Now, I don't want to jump to conclusions, but let's just say that Priya is not a name I hear often in our house. No, Priya is not one of the regulars in my kitchen, no matter how good her intentions might be with all her helping hands. In fact, Priya is someone I had never met until now. Why didn't he say anything about her if she was just a colleague?

Suddenly, my thoughts began to race faster than a pot of boiling water left unattended. Who was this Priya? Why was she "looking for" my husband? What kind of "looking" was happening here? Many scenarios played out in my mind, each one more absurd than the last, but nothing made sense.

I took a deep breath and tried to focus. He's a good man. He's not that type of man. I'd just wait. I would simply wait for him to come home and explain, like the rational, calm, and level-headed woman I am.

But then again, maybe I was wrong. Maybe this was no simple case of "I'm just late from work." No, this was a new wrinkle in our comfortable life. The first crack in the Meera-brand perfection I'd so carefully crafted over the years.

As I set the table again, this time for one, I wondered: Could it be true? Could my husband, Raghavan, be involved with another woman?

I wasn't sure. But I wasn't stupid either.

I decided right then and there that I would find out. Because, you know, nothing says "I love my family" more than playing the role of a detective while simultaneously ensuring dinner doesn't burn.

And so, I began to plan. The search for reality had begun.

10

The Unraveling

The door creaked open with an all-too-familiar sound; I hadn't realized I'd been holding my breath for it until I heard it. It was him, My Raghavan. Even the simple act of hearing him walk in brings a sense of relief. He seemed very tired.

Without even looking at me, he just walked into the bedroom, saying, "I'm tired; let me take a shower." The house was silent, except for the ticking of the wall clock and the sound of the fan spinning above me. I sat at the kitchen table grabbing a cup of tea, hoping it would ease my headache, but it failed miserably.

Since BBC Aunty had mentioned her name, I hadn't told anyone. Not even my children, not yet. They were innocent, untouched by the possibility of betrayal. But me? I was branded already. I had already experienced this new reality's sting. All that remained was the rubble of my own naive confidence after Raghavan unexpectedly fell from the pedestal I had placed him on.

I was a hopeless romantic, pouring my heart into planning his birthdays and making every Valentine's Day memorable, even if it always felt one-sided. Yet, I loved every moment of it. For me, it was about making him feel special and showing him the love I hoped to receive in return. Perhaps, in a way, I treated him the way I wished to be treated. He never appeared expressive or interested. He always struck me as someone with a strong, realistic face, someone firmly anchored in realism and pragmatism.

My legs were heavy with the weight of what was to come, so I stood slowly. The world outside appeared muted, as if I were underwater and the stillness of my own heart buried my thoughts. Once I poured my love into every meal, my kitchen felt like a war zone. I needed to know the truth. The wall clock began to tick louder, akin to an unstoppable countdown. The truth, once revealed, would change everything. But I had no choice. I had to uncover it.

I reached for Raghavan's phone and started scrolling through the messages. I could feel my heartbeat in my throat. The messages were too many to ignore. Words of affection. Plans for late-night meetings. The moments spent and a promise to meet soon. I could feel the ground beneath me shift, the foundation of my life cracking open like a poorly baked cake. I had to confront him. But how? What words could I say that would undo the hurt already carved into my chest? How could I look at the man I had spent years building a life with and tell him I knew what he had done?

I didn't want to cry. However, I could sense the tears threatening, as if they were about to burst. Instead, with trembling hands, I placed the phone down and walked, my feet moving naturally. I needed to think—to gather my strength—but all I could think about was how fragile everything felt now. How foolish I had been to trust so completely. The weight of my own ignorance crushed me.

Raghavan's voice, once so familiar and comforting, now seemed distant. My mind replayed the countless small moments, the smiles he had given me, the promises he had made, each one now hollow, tainted with the knowledge that they had been said while he had already begun to betray me. I waited for him to explain. But deep down, I knew. I knew that no explanation could undo the betrayal. I was uncertain about how to confront him and the aftermath. I sat in silence, wondering how many more of these quiet moments I would have to endure before I could face the truth. The truth that would shatter everything.

11 The Q&A

Raghavan said, "Serve the food. Need to sleep early." The voice, once soothing to my ears, now evoked a mixture of uncertainty, resentment, and deep, gnawing anguish that I could not quite place. With my back to him, I stood in the living room using the edge of the chair for balance. I had made no attempt to hide the fact that I was waiting. I anticipated his words, anticipating his self-explanation.

"Meera?" His voice sounded more tired than usual. He wore the mask of a busy man, always caught in meetings, rushing from one project to the next. Though inside, my heart was pounding, I turned slowly and tried to retain my calm. His face was filled with confusion as he sat at the dining table. His eyes, once so full of warmth when they looked at me, now seemed distant, as though they were looking for a way out.

"Where were you?" I asked.

He took a deep breath, trying to avoid eye contact. "I'm sorry, Meera," he said, stepping into the living room. "I know I've been late these past few days, but work is very hectic. You know how it is. Big projects, deadlines. It's been overwhelming." Slowly, I nodded, but I could feel the walls starting to crack inside me. I just couldn't understand the lie he was telling me. It looked like he had used them too many times to hide something that didn't belong in our house. "And what about last night?" I asked, unable to stop myself. "You promised to come home at seven, but you didn't. You didn't even call. I waited. And then, I found out you were with Priya. I heard she was on the lookout for you today. It must be pleasant to have someone who is so eager to find you, don't you think?"

My voice weakened slightly at the last part, but it was still loud enough to make him flinch. "Meera, it's not what you think," he said, his tone turning defensive, almost frantic. "Priya... she's just a colleague. We've been working on a project together for months. You understand the nature of work. At times, we find ourselves stalled; at other times, we must revisit matters." I could feel the words, "just a colleague," cutting through me. My breath caught in my throat. "A colleague? Really?" The bitterness in my voice was obvious. "A colleague who texts you at all hours? A colleague who you meet in private? That's your excuse, Raghavan? Is that what you expect me to believe?"

He looked at me, his eyes wide with guilt. "Meera, I swear. Please don't!"

"Don't lie to me. I've seen the messages. I've seen everything. You are a liar, Raghavan. You broke me." His face turned pale. For a moment, there was silence between us, a silence that felt suffocating; his lies had finally caught up with him. His hand dropped to his side. He sat as if struck by lightning.

"I didn't mean for it to go this far," he murmured after a long pause. "I never wanted to hurt you. But it just happened. It was a big mistake. I'm sorry, Meera." The words were like a slap to my face. Of course, it wasn't supposed to be. I had built this life and this marriage on trust, on the idea that we were partners in everything. And now, the very foundation of everything I had known was falling apart.

"I'm at a loss for words, Raghavan." I can't help but feel the tears that had been on the verge of falling finally trickle down my cheeks. "You've shattered my soul, and I don't think I can ever look at you the same way again." He reached out to touch me, but I stepped back. "No. You don't get to fix this with an apology. Not after everything."

For a moment, he just stood there, his hand frozen in mid-air; the distance between us was more than just physical. It was the distance that only betrayal could create, and I knew, deep down, that we might never bridge it again.

12

The Cracks Beneath the Surface

I didn't know how much longer I could stay in this house The house, where Raghavan and I had shared so many meals and quiet evenings with only the hum of the ceiling fan to keep us company, was now a place of betrayal. Now, though, it seemed like the whole house was talking about betrayal. How quickly things had gone wrong was shown by how strange things that used to be were now.

I couldn't sleep that night. I stayed thinking about what Raghavan said and what we didn't talk about during our conversation. I had heard him say sorry. He looked sorry in my eyes, or at least I think he did. Things didn't feel the same, though. He didn't make me feel better or warmer when he touched me. It looked like everything had been cleared out, leaving only the ghost of what it used to be.

I stayed up in bed all night long, gazing at the ceiling and the way the shadows cast by the tree outside danced on the walls. It seemed like the night went on for much too long. Tears were welling up in my eyes, but I would not allow them to fall. No more. Crying wouldn't make a difference. There would still be a huge void in my life that it couldn't fill.

The following day, Raghavan made an effort to appear normal. With his trademark grin intact, he descended the steps before me, as if he hadn't just destroyed my faith in humanity. He made small talk, asking me how the kids were, what was for breakfast, and things that should have mattered, but in that moment, felt so far removed from the truth. I couldn't bring myself to respond the way I always had. I couldn't act like nothing had happened.

I told Raghavan in a low voice, "I can't do this. There's no way I can keep acting like everything is okay like nothing has changed. It's not possible to erase what happened last night or what has been going on for months." He looked at me, his face filled with confusion and frustration.

"Meera, please."

"No, Raghavan. I need to think. I need space to think about what you've done. I need space to figure out whether this marriage is even something I want anymore." My voice cracked on the last sentence, and for the first time, I saw real panic in his eyes. But I had already made up my mind. I didn't know what would happen in the days ahead, but I knew one thing for sure: I couldn't continue to live in this lie.

The house, once a symbol of safety and comfort, now resembled a prison. It took several days for me to understand what was happening to me. I made an effort to avoid Raghavan by immersing myself in my thoughts. I was too scared to face him because his excuses and empty promises were too much for me to handle. They were hollow and meaningless words. The trust was lost, regardless of how hard he tried to defend his behavior or how many times he vowed that it wouldn't happen again.

Furthermore, it is very difficult to regain trust after it has been lost. I found myself thinking about Priya. She was still a shadow in my mind, an unknown figure I couldn't seem to shake. How long had this affair been going on? How many lies had Raghavan told to keep it hidden? My heart was heavy with the realization that the guy I had given everything to had devoted his love and his time to someone else.

The days blended into one another, each feeling heavier than the previous. I tried to keep wearing a mask for the kids, but they could see something was wrong. Lakshmi, who was usually quick to ask about my day, became quieter. Arun seemed to notice that I wasn't smiling as much as I used to. They didn't know what was happening, and I didn't know how to explain it to them without breaking their hearts.

And then, one evening, as I sat alone in the living room, I realized something. As much as the pain hurt, as much as it felt like my world was crumbling, I didn't need to wait for Raghavan to fix things. I didn't need him to apologize or promise that things would be different. What I needed, what I had always needed, was to be strong enough to fix myself. Raghavan might have betrayed me, but I wasn't going to let him take my dignity, my sense of self, with him. I knew I couldn't continue to live in this suffocating environment, but I had no idea what the future contained. I did not need to explain myself to him. I owed no one an explanation for the decisions I would make going forward. In reality, I had always been sufficient. That was something I needed to remind myself of.

13

The Choice

The morning light crept through the curtains, gentle and innocent, as if the outside world was unaware of the storm gathering behind these walls. I'd spent the whole night going over every imaginable situation in my head, but I still felt no closer to an answer.

I had cried, I had raged, I had shut myself away from Raghavan's apologies and pleading eyes. But now, the silence seemed to press down on me harder than ever, and I knew it was time to make a choice.

The children were at school, their joyful laughter and lively chatter now replaced by the soft hum of the house, a place that had been my universe for so many years. However, today, it felt unrecognizable to me. Today, it felt chilly and strange. It appeared as though I had stepped into another world.

Standing in the kitchen, I looked at the well-placed dishes—plates of dosa and chutney, the breakfast Raghavan had often complimented. Still, the thought of making him breakfast this morning—of serving him the dish I had thoughtfully created—felt almost unbearable. The lie that had cast a cloud over the life we had built together was no longer something I could ignore, but he seemed to be accepting it with every bite.

I could hear Raghavan moving around, but being around him didn't make me feel better like it used to. The man I had trusted, the man I had spent years with, was no longer the one I knew. He had become a stranger, someone I didn't understand, someone who had taken my trust and care and shattered it.

He had broken something in me, something deep and unspoken. And I realized that I couldn't go back to the way things were. I couldn't simply erase the knowledge of his infidelity. It would hang over us like a shadow, a constant reminder of what we had, what I thought we had, was never as solid as I believed.

The thought of leaving him, of walking away from the life we had built, seemed both impossible and inevitable. How did you leave someone who was still your husband, who still wore the same face and spoke the same words? But at that moment, I knew. I had to give up the delusion. In the back of the house, I went to the small room I had turned into a study. Every time I went there, I could be alone with my thoughts and forget about the stresses of everyday life. I hadn't been in there in weeks, or maybe even months. I needed clarity today, though. I had to think about it.

I sat down at the desk and got the pen and paper I had left there a long time ago. The outside world seemed far away, and writing tuned out the sounds of everyday

life. Writing down everything I felt was important to me because I had been holding it in for a long time. I had to face the truth about what I was going through.
I wrote mindfully and slowly as if every word would confirm my choice.

I have always devoted myself to Raghavan and this family. Where does it leave me, though? I have made every effort to be the best version of myself as a wife and mother. But now my broken heart is all that's left of me. I cherished him. I had faith in him. But after everything he's done, can I still love him? Can I forgive him, or will I always be haunted by this betrayal?

My pen hovered above the page as I stopped. In my hands, the words seemed heavy, as if they were carrying a burden I wasn't sure I could handle. However, I was aware that I could no longer deny the reality. I had clung for so long to the notion of us, to our ideal marriage, to the life I believed we led. However, it was all based on a shaky foundation. Something that was irreparably cracked.

I knew I had made my decision when I eventually put the pen down. However, I was not yet aware of the implications of that decision. I wasn't sure whether I could abandon all I had put so much effort into creating.

The thought of leaving Raghavan was terrifying. I couldn't imagine what life would be like without him, without the routine we had established. But could I live with the constant hurt? Could I continue to act as though I was part of something that had already failed?

It was time for me to talk to him to clarify everything. I couldn't continue to avoid the reality. It was important to face the grief, the falsehoods, and the betrayal. For me to heal, I needed closure, whether or not it came from him.

I heard footsteps approaching the room, and I stood up quickly, stuffing the paper into the drawer. Raghavan's face appeared in the doorway a moment later, his eyes cautious but hopeful.

Looking into his eyes, I felt heavy inside because of what I had to say. "I'm done acting, Raghavan," I whispered. The words hit me hard in the heart and lifted a weight from my shoulders. "Let's talk. I can no longer do this."

He raised his hand to talk, but I stopped him. "No more stalling. Don't lie anymore."

There was a long pause between us. It was full of all the things we hadn't said to each other. During that moment of quiet, I knew what I had to do. I wasn't sure what the future held, but I knew I couldn't keep giving up my integrity for someone who had already given up on me.

I needed to take back control of my life.

14

The Confrontation

The home was filled with a burden of unspoken words, feelings, and regrets that hovered heavily like an unmoving storm cloud. Raghavan faced me, his expression a mix of worry and a trace of shame. He had no idea what was going to happen. Maybe he did, though. The focus had shifted away from us. My future, dignity, and peace were at stake.

"Meera, can we please just talk?" Raghavan spoke in a more soothing tone, but his words were ultimately inconsolable. Not for me, not anymore.

I didn't want to hear it. I didn't want his promises or his excuses. I had spent years listening to them, and where had that gotten me? His words were just empty sounds now. I had already heard it all: work pressures, misunderstandings, a "moment of weakness", the kind of explanations that only served to make me feel small, to make me feel like my feelings weren't valid. No more.

"I don't need explanations, Raghavan," I said, my voice steady but heavy. "What I need is honesty. The truth. And

I don't think you're capable of giving me that."

Raghavan blinked, looking like I had slapped him. But I couldn't care. Not anymore. "Let me clarify. I—I've been confused. Meera, I really didn't want this to happen," he muttered, his breaths coming out hurriedly. "It was my fault. A huge mistake. I assure you, Priya is over."

"Are you seriously saying that I am unaware of that?" My hands were trembling as I stepped forward, but I finally snapped. "You think that just because you've decided to end it now, it changes anything? Do you think I can just forget the months of lies, the secret texts, the late nights, and the things you said to her that you never said to me?"

The silence that followed felt suffocating. Raghavan opened his mouth as if to speak, but I cut him off.

"No more lies. I've been holding on, hoping that you would see the damage, that you'd wake up and realize what you've done. But this... this isn't something you can just fix with words, Raghavan."

He took a step closer, his eyes desperate. "Meera, I'm sorry. I know what I've done to you. I've hurt you, and I'll do anything to make it right. Please don't leave me."

I felt the tears welling up, but I held them back, refusing to let him see how much he had already torn me apart. "I'm not leaving you just because of one mistake, Raghavan. I'm leaving you because you've made a choice. You've chosen her. You've chosen to betray me, to betray the trust we built together. And you've done it repeatedly.

I can't do this anymore."

His face contorted, a mix of shock and realization. The truth was setting in, but it was too late. I had been patient, waiting for the man I loved to come back to me. But the man I once knew was gone. In his place stood someone who had not only betrayed me but had disrespected everything I stood for. I was no longer that woman who would just forgive and forget. I had lost too much of myself in this marriage to keep pretending that everything was okay.

"Meera, please," he whispered, his voice breaking now. "I love you. I need you."

For a brief moment, I saw the man I had married, the man I had shared so many dreams with. But even that wasn't enough to make me forget the hurt, the hollow feeling that had consumed me ever since I found out the truth.

"You don't love me," I said softly but firmly. "You love the idea of me. You love the version of me that was easy to manipulate, who was willing to put up with your lies. But I'm done being that woman. I deserve better than this."

I could see tears in his eyes, but it didn't move me anymore. I had cried enough for both of us.

"I need time, Raghavan. I need space to think. Not for us, but for me." I took a deep breath. "And you need to leave. I can't live with you under the same roof anymore. Not after everything."

He stood there, frozen, like the ground had been ripped out from under him. But the truth was, there was no place for him in my life anymore. And I was finally, finally ready to take the first step into the life that was mine, not the one he had stolen from me.

“I’ll move out,” he said, his voice quieter now, as though he had given up. “I don’t know what else to say. I’m sorry, Meera.”

“You already said it,” I replied coldly. “But it’s too late.”

I turned and walked out of the room, my heart pounding, but there was a lightness to my steps that hadn’t been there before. This wasn’t the end of my pain, but it was the end of my suffering at his hands. I was finally free, even if it meant walking into the unknown.

15

The Aftermath

The days following Raghavan's departure were a blur of emotions. I moved through the motions of daily life: waking up, feeding the kids, and making sure they were ready for school. But my heart wasn't in it. I was running on autopilot, a shell of the woman I used to be, and though I smiled at my children, I knew they could sense something was wrong. I wasn't the same Meera they had grown up with.

I thought the moment he left would bring relief, but instead, it felt like a weight had been added to my shoulders.

The silence in the house was deafening. At first, I couldn't stand it. The quiet that had once been comforting now felt suffocating, every corner of the house echoing the absence of a life I had once known.

The hardest part wasn't the absence of Raghavan. No, the hardest part was realizing that I had built my identity around someone who no longer deserved it. I had been so caught up in the idea of being a good wife and a good

mother that I had forgotten to take care of myself. I had given so much, but what had I received in return?
My friends, those few I had kept in touch with, rallied around me. They called, they came by, and they tried to comfort me, but I couldn't let them in. Not completely.

How could I explain to them that after all these years, I had been living with someone who wasn't who I thought he was? How could I make them understand the profound sense of betrayal that gnawed at me? No matter how much they reassured me that I was strong, that I would be okay, I knew that strength came from within, and I wasn't sure I had it yet.

One evening, as I sat on the couch, flipping absentmindedly through a magazine, I caught a glimpse of a photo on the coffee table of Raghavan and me at our wedding. We were so young, so hopeful. I hadn't realized how much I had changed until that moment. It was like looking at a version of myself I no longer recognized.

I leaned forward, reaching for the photo. There was no hate in my heart, only a quiet, aching sorrow. The Meera in the photo was happy. She trusted, she loved, she believed. That woman was gone now, though. And it hurt to say it, but the life I had built with Raghavan was just a lie. It was like a house of cards that fell apart when I found out the truth.

That's where I put the picture back. I was no longer interested in the past. I needed to move on but didn't know how.

I met with a counselor the next day, which was something I never thought I'd do. I had always been proud of how well I could handle things by myself, but I knew I couldn't handle this on my own. It was too hard on my emotions, and the guilt that came with ending my marriage hurt more than I wanted to speak about. I needed to talk to someone who wasn't emotionally involved and could help me figure out what was going on.

It made me feel like somebody else walking into an unfamiliar setting when I got to the counseling center. The walls were a soft blue and green color, and the air smelled like lavender. I sat down in the waiting room. It was so quiet that it was almost painful, and my mind was rushing. What was I doing here? Would this make any difference? Would talking to a stranger really help?

The counselor's name was Anita. She was warm and kind, and she asked me to share my story. For the first time in many days, I opened up about everything: the years of sacrifice, the quiet unraveling of my marriage, the way I had allowed Raghavan to take so much from me without questioning it. And as I spoke, I realized something important: I had never given myself the space to feel what I was feeling. I had buried it all beneath the responsibilities of being a wife, a mother, and a caretaker. But now, in that small office with Anita, I was finally giving myself permission to grieve.

"Meera," Anita said after a long silence, "You've been through something incredibly painful. But the important thing now is not to punish yourself. Your worth was never tied to your marriage. It's tied to who you are as a person, as a mother, as a woman. You need to heal, but you need to heal on your terms."

Her words settled in my chest, and for the first time, I felt a spark of something, hope maybe. Maybe I could heal. Maybe I could find myself again. It wouldn't be easy. It wouldn't be quick. But I didn't need to have all the answers right now.

As I walked out of the counseling center, I felt a faint stir within me, a small spark of the woman I once was, before Raghavan, before the pain. I wasn't sure what the future held, but for the first time in a long while, I felt like I had the strength to face it.

16

The Road to Rediscovery

Life had changed since Raghavan moved out a month ago. The world seemed to be bearing down on my chest at first, and then a strange sort of silence had descended. When it all stopped, I saw how much I depended on the commotion, the daily grind, the disputes, and the never-ending barrage of demands. The only sounds left were my own breathing, the faint hum of the fan in the background, and the occasional chirp of birds outside.

Anita and I met once a week. More than anything, she helped me put my feelings into words. She was patient and compassionate. Every session seemed like a tiny step closer to understanding my own suffering and gaining clarity.

It wasn't that I was "moving on" just yet; I wasn't sure if I would ever be able to do that, but I was learning to give myself permission to feel. It took some time, but I learned to forgive myself for not being the woman I thought I should be.

The stillness in the home would sometimes ring louder than ever as I lay awake at night and stared at the ceiling. I missed the old Meera, the one who believed in a happily ever after, the one who laughed and enjoyed the small things in life. I missed the idea of who I thought I was and who I thought I would be with Raghavan. But that Meera, that version of me, had been buried under years of compromise, of being the "perfect" wife and mother. It was time for her to come back if she still existed under the rubble.

I sat at the easel, waiting for me to recall how to use a brush, and spent time rediscovering my love of painting, which I had given up after getting married. I felt as though the vibrant colors were a tiny protest against the grayness of my surroundings. I was too shy and unsure at first, but as the paint began to flow, I felt a little more of who I really was emerge with each stroke.

I was painting in the little room at the back of the house one evening when Arun entered with a puzzled look on his face. He had been quiet lately, and though I knew he missed his father, I was glad that he had stayed with me through this. He was old enough to understand more than I realized, and his silent presence comforted me.

"Mom, you look different," he said. I stopped mid-stroke, wiping my hands on a cloth. "Different how?"

"Like... you're not so sad anymore," he said, offering me a shy smile. "I like it. It's nice to see you happy again." His words hit me like a wave, and I couldn't stop the tear that slipped down my cheek. I quickly wiped it away, but

Arun's eyes were sharp. He didn't say anything more, but I knew he understood. Maybe not all of it, but enough. I pulled him into a hug, holding him tightly. "I'm trying, Arun. I really am." It was moments like these that made me realize how much I had been missing. I had spent so much time being consumed by Raghavan's betrayal, by my own pain, that I had forgotten how much my children needed me to be present, to show them that we could still have joy, even in the midst of heartbreak.
Several weeks down the road, I made up my mind to do something else. I had always wanted to attend a cookery class, and I finally got the chance. Although I had always enjoyed cooking, it turned into a chore as the years passed. I felt obligated to make each meal like it was a chore to do. I wanted to take it back for myself now, though. I didn't want to cook because I had to, but because I liked it.

I experienced the same old anxiety on the first day of class since I was going somewhere new, meeting new people, and doing something for which I wasn't sure I was prepared. But the instructor, a woman named Lilly, was warm and welcoming, and the other students were all enthusiastic in their own right. The smell of fresh spices, the chopping of vegetables, the hum of conversation—it felt like a world I hadn't allowed myself to enter in so long. I was chopping onions and tomatoes when Lilly shared with us the wonders of food and how it could be a kind of self-care and a way to show love to oneself and others. She smiled and said, "Perfection isn't important. It's about joy. It's about being present in the moment and savoring the process."

For the first time in a long while, I felt connected to something outside of my pain, outside of my guilt. I felt like I was rediscovering a part of myself that had been buried. It wasn't the same as me before—I had changed. I wasn't the woman I had been when I married Raghavan. But maybe that was okay. Maybe, in the mess of it all, I would find something better. As I left the class that evening, carrying a bag of ingredients to make a simple curry, I felt a sense of accomplishment, of having done something for me, of having taken a step in the right direction. Even though the road ahead was long and scary, I wasn't afraid of it anymore. One step at a time, I was learning to walk it.

I never thought my life would turn out this way. One year ago, I was just a woman caught up in the day-to-day grind, trying to keep a failing marriage together, masking my suffering behind smiles, and putting all of my energy into cooking because it was the only thing that made sense. Cooking has, however, become my rebirth, my means of taking control, and, to my surprise, a business.

The concept was basic: what if I shared my recipes? What if I used food as a means of sharing my rediscovery? At first, it was nothing more than a few pictures on Instagram—just me experimenting in the kitchen, trying out new dishes, and posting them with the occasional caption about how I was learning to heal, one curry at a time. But something amazing happened. People began to connect with my story. They resonated with the idea that food could be more than just nourishment; it could be a symbol of transformation.

And then came the message. A food blogger, someone I didn't even know, asked if he could feature me on his page. It seemed like a joke to me at first. Me? Featured? However, everything changed the instant I said yes. The post became widely shared. People all across my city and even outside of it suddenly wanted to know who I was. They were interested in my recipes. They were interested in my narrative.

As any intelligent woman would, I took advantage of the situation. I began a blog where I shared my experiences as well as recipes. How I used food to find healing and how I transformed my suffering into something meaningful. Not only did I write about perfecting my dosa and sambar skills, but I also wrote about healing from betrayal and finding happiness in the little things. And what do you know? It was successful.

Eventually, event managers and businesses started getting in touch to work together. I was invited to do live cooking demonstrations at local food festivals. I even started offering private classes where people could learn to make my favorite dishes and, if they wanted, talk about life, healing, and starting over. I wasn't just a cook anymore. I was a storyteller. A woman who had turned her heartbreak into something that brought joy to others.

What truly blew my mind, though, was when I started offering virtual cooking classes. I wasn't sure if people would sign up after all; I was just a regular woman who'd been through a lot. I did it anyway, though. And people answered. In addition to learning how to cook, many of the men and women in my workshops wanted to learn how to live a purposeful life despite hardship.

At first, it seemed unreal. Me? A woman in business? A popular person on social media? A year ago, I would have laughed at the notion. But it seemed right somehow. Speaking about food, life, and healing made me feel as if I was supposed to be here. The encouragement I received from my growing community was overwhelming. Not only were they interested in my food, but they were also interested in knowing me. For the person I was at the time.

People invited me to give speeches at events that support women's rights. In those speeches, I shared about how I got through my problems. And every time I stepped on stage, I felt so thankful. Not only for the acknowledgment but also for the path that led me to this point. These days, my business is more than simply food. It's about spreading a hopeful message. It's about encouraging people to discover their own power like I did.

Really, it's funny. After my world was destroyed, I set out on this trip to recover and rediscover peace. And I've discovered so much more since then. I've discovered a group of individuals that share my viewpoint. I've found a career I never expected. And most importantly, I've found myself. Cooking became my escape, my therapy, and now it's my purpose. And as for Raghavan? Well, his role in my story is over, but I've never been more grateful for everything that happened, because it led me here to a life I never knew I was capable of.

Funny how life works, isn't it?

17

The Unexpected Encounter

The sky was dark and felt like it was going to rain that afternoon. I was waiting for my coffee order in front of my favorite coffee shop in the late afternoon. The light made the streets look like they were already wet. I took the afternoon off to spend time with myself. There were no kids or work, just a few hours of peace and quiet to enjoy my own company.

When the door opened, it chimed, and I looked up from the book I was reading without giving it much thought. It was Raghavan, who walked into the cafe like he owned it. A small jolt went through my heart, like an automatic response I couldn't stop. It had been almost six months since he packed up and left. Since then, I hadn't seen him. I wasn't ready for this.

As soon as his eyes met mine, he looked stunned. We stood there for a moment, with only a few tables between us and the regulars' chatter in the background. There was an uncomfortable quiet between us as if the weight of everything we didn't say was like a cloud in the air.

His presence and the situation surprised me. Getting through everything had been tough, but seeing him here made me feel everything again. I was mad. It made me hurt. Still, something else was happening that I wasn't ready for.

"Meera..." It sounded like he wasn't sure how to talk to me after everything that had happened.

I quickly gathered my things and stood up because I wanted to get away from the uncomfortable tension that had built up between us. What I didn't need was to talk to him again and say something I might later regret or let him off the hook again. But he took a step forward with a sober gaze. "Can we talk?"

I hesitated. It wasn't just about what he had done anymore; it was about whether I was strong enough to confront it. Whether I was ready to face the person who had broken me and see what, if anything, was left.

I spoke with a strong voice, even though I was scared, "Raghavan, there's nothing to talk about. You made your choice, and I did too. You can't change that with what you say."

He winced as if the words hurt more than I meant them to. I no longer cared, though. The focus wasn't on him or his shame. It was about me taking charge of my own story.

He said with a little crack in his voice, "I know I've hurt you. I'm sorry. I didn't mean for things to turn out this way."

"Sorry?" I asked again, shaking my head. "That word has no meaning anymore, Raghavan. You were sorry while you were with her, weren't you? You were sorry when you lied to my face, when you broke our family, and now you're sorry because I've stopped taking your crap."

The words were harsher than I meant, but they had been sitting inside me for so long, festering in the silence between us. For once, I allowed myself to speak freely, without concern for his feelings or for what he might say in return.

"Meera, please," he said, stepping closer. "I don't expect you to forgive me. I just... I need you to understand that I've been a fool. That I never wanted to lose you. I never wanted any of this."

I looked at him for a long moment, wondering what it would be like to go back to the days when I believed in him completely, when I trusted him with my heart. But that Meera was gone. I had spent so much of my life believing that love was enough to fix anything. But love without respect, without trust, was nothing more than a hollow shell.

"You can't undo what's been done, Raghavan," I said, finally softening. "You broke me. You broke us. I will never forget that. I'll never be the woman I used to be again."

There was silence again for a moment, and the air between us felt thick and heavy. Perhaps seeing the gravity of his deeds, he stood there with his gloomy eyes and stooped shoulders.

He said in a voice that was barely above a whisper, "I'm sorry for everything. I'd change it if I could. I'd do anything to fix things."

There was no magic fix, no quick solution. There was only the reality of the mess he had made and the work it would take to heal from it.

He said in a soft voice, "I hope you can forgive me someday."

"But I forgive you already. Not for you. For me."

Raghavan did not say anything further. He did nothing but stand there and look at me with a sad and sorry face. For once, I didn't feel the rage or grief that had been my regular companions for so long. There was instead a feeling of calm. I felt free and at peace.
I stood there and watched him leave the coffee shop. As he walked away, the hurt of the past started to leave me. I had no idea what would happen next. I knew I would be okay for the first time in a long time.

18

Ready for the World

So here I am, the Meera you didn't see coming, running a successful business, teaching the world how to cook, how to heal, and, more importantly, how to live life on *their* own terms. To be honest, sometimes I look at myself in the mirror and think, "Is this really me?" But then, I remember, of course, it's me! It's always been me. Somewhere under all those layers of wife duties, motherly responsibilities, and societal expectations, *she* was always waiting to emerge.

I've got a pretty good routine now. Morning yoga, a couple of hours of work on my blog, managing my cooking classes, and, when the mood strikes, hosting live cooking sessions where I basically share my life story and stir pots of curry. That's the funny thing—I don't even have to try. People relate to the *me* that I've become. They don't just want a recipe, they want the recipe for how to live.

But of course, things don't always go as planned. Just when I thought I had everything in place, life had to throw in a little surprise. And guess who walked in with that surprise? None other than Raghavan, my dear ex-husband, the man who had turned my world upside down and then promptly walked out of it, probably looking for greener pastures, or maybe just better Wi-Fi.

I was sitting in my office (yes, I have an office now, don't ask me how that happened) going through some orders for a special event when the doorbell rang. I opened the door expecting the delivery guy with my much-needed supply of spices, but instead, there stood Raghavan, looking lost, with that sheepish expression he always wore when he thought he could talk his way out of something.

"Meera, we need to talk," he said, standing there as if he had just realized how terribly wrong he had been.

I almost laughed. Talk? What more is there to say?

"Go on, Raghavan," I said, leaning against the doorframe, my arms crossed. "Talk. I'm all ears."

He shuffled his feet, looking everywhere but at me. "Look, I know I messed up. I've been thinking a lot about... about everything. And I..."

Before he could finish, I cut him off. "Raghavan, do you know what the problem is? The problem is not that you messed up. The problem is you never realized that I had to get up every time I fell. While you were out playing hero with your 'other woman,' I was here, building a life from scratch, teaching my children that resilience doesn't come from apologies, it comes from actions."

His face looked as if I had slapped him with a wet towel, but I wasn't done. "And now, here you are, all dramatic, trying to talk me into a 'second chance'. Newsflash, Anbu Thozha, the only second chance you get is when I serve you a second helping of *kootu* at one of my cooking classes."

Raghavan opened his mouth, probably to say something to save face, but I was done. I'd heard enough. The truth was, I didn't need his validation anymore. I didn't need him to give me permission to live my life.

"Raghavan," I said with a grin, "here's a simple piece of advice. There's no rewind in life, and trust me, this is not a scene that you can just walk back into. You can't control the plot anymore. And Like Rajinikanth says, 'En vazhi, thani vazhi!' (I'm still unsure of what I was thinking when I used that dialog)."

Raghavan blinked. A beat of silence. Then he awkwardly nodded, probably trying to process the whole 'Rajinikanth moment' I had just thrown at him. But I wasn't waiting around for him to figure out his emotions.

"Good luck, Raghavan," I said with a smile that could only be described as the one I'd been practicing in the mirror for weeks, one that reflected confidence, freedom, and an irrepressible sense of self-worth. "You'll need it. But just know this, my life is better without your drama. And if you ever feel the urge to join my cooking class, you're always welcome. You were a chapter, Raghavan, not the whole book. I've already written the next one, and you're not in it."

And with that, I closed the door behind him, feeling lighter than I had in months.

www.ingramcontent.com/pod-product-compliance
Lightning Source LLC
LaVergne TN
LVHW041232150826
845673LV00008B/2364

* 9 7 9 8 8 9 6 9 9 1 1 5 1 *